# ONE EYE, TWO EYES, THREE EYES

*A Hutzul Tale*

## retold by Eric A. Kimmel
## illustrated by Dirk Zimmer

Holiday House/New York

To Colleen and Patrick
E. A. K.

To Vivian
D. Z.

Library of Congress Cataloging-in-Publication Data
Kimmel, Eric A.
One Eye, Two Eyes, Three Eyes: a Hutzul tale / retold by Eric A. Kimmel; illustrated by Dirk Zimmer. — 1st ed.
p.     cm.
Summary: To honor her father's promise, a beautiful young girl
agrees to become the slave of a witch and her two daughters,
enduring their cruelty with the help of her talking pet goat.
ISBN 0-8234-1183-4
[1. Hutsuls—Folklore.   2. Folklore—Ukraine.]   I. Zimmer, Dirk,
ill.   II. Title.
PZ8.1.K567On     1996     94-42362     CIP     AC
398.2—dc20

# AUTHOR'S NOTE

The theme of the person who makes a foolish vow that must be redeemed with a beloved child can be found in many cultures. One example is the biblical story of "Jephthah's Daughter" from the Book of Judges (11:29–40).

There are many versions of "One Eye, Two Eyes, Three Eyes," including one in *Grimm's Fairy Tales.* I based this retelling on a story I heard originally from my grandmother. My grandmother came from the Ukrainian town of Kolomyya, which is in the heart of Hutzul country. Hutzuls are a Ukrainian-speaking ethnic group of obscure origins who live in the Carpathian mountains.

Elizabeth Wayland Barber includes an interesting comment about spinning nettles in her book *Women's Work: The First 2,000 Years.* Spinning nettles into thread sounds like torture, but it can be done if one knows how. The wild nettles are plucked by hand, taking care to move the hand up the stalk so that the stingers lie flat. They are "retted"—soaked and left to rot—which removes the stingers and plant matter, exposing the long fibers. These can be spun and woven just like linen, which is prepared from flax in the same way. According to Professor Barber, nettle thread produces a smooth, lustrous fabric, well worth the extra trouble and an occasional sting.

Once upon a time a Hutzul and his daughter lived high in the Carpathian mountains on the edge of a deep, dark forest. Every morning the Hutzul went into the forest to gather moss, roots, and lichens which his daughter made into poultices and teas for curing aches, fevers, and other ailments.

One day, while seeking certain healing mosses, the Hutzul lost his way. As he wandered through the forest, he came upon an old woman bent over a fire.

"Grandmother, take pity on me. Show me the way out of the forest," the Hutzul said.

The old woman looked up. The Hutzul realized at once she was a witch, for instead of two eyes, she had three; two on either side of her nose, and a third set squarely in the middle of her forehead.

"What will you give me if I do?" the witch asked.

"I have nothing to give," the Hutzul answered.

"You have more than you think," the witch told him. "Promise me your most precious possession, and I will help you."

The Hutzul agreed. After all, what did he own that was worth anything except a china plate and two brass candlesticks?

The witch showed the Hutzul a hidden path that wound behind the trees. She said to him, "This path will lead you home. Tomorrow morning, leave your most precious possession by the edge of the forest, and I will come for it. Don't forget your promise."

The Hutzul followed the path to his own front door. His daughter Larissa ran out to greet him.

"Father, you are home at last! I was so worried. What would I do without you?"

"What would I do without you, dearest Larissa?" the Hutzul said. "You are my most precious possession."

Too late, he realized what sort of bargain he had made. He had promised his daughter, his most precious possession, to a witch.

The Hutzul told Larissa what he had done.

"Never fear, Father," Larissa said. "Heaven will watch over me, and I will take along my little white goat as my companion. The witch will not object to that."

The goat had been Larissa's friend and guardian since childhood. Though none but Larissa knew it, the goat possessed the power of speech.

Larissa rose before dawn. She and the goat walked to the edge of the forest.

The sun had barely cleared the horizon when the witch appeared, her three eyes blinking in the sunlight.

"The Hutzul has kept his word, and thrown in a goat for good measure!" the witch exclaimed. "Come with me, dearie." She grasped Larissa's hand and led her into the forest. The goat followed.

They traveled along secret paths until they came to the witch's house. The witch's two daughters rushed out to meet them. These girls were more hideous than their mother. The elder had one eye in the middle of her forehead. The younger had two: one on top of the other.

"Fresh meat! Fresh meat!" they cried, snatching at the goat and Larissa. The witch slapped their hands away.

"These two can serve us better than that," she said. "The goat will give us milk, and the girl will be our slave."

Larissa toiled from dawn to dusk for the old witch Three Eyes and her daughters, One Eye and Two Eyes. She cooked and washed, wove and spun, brewed and baked with never a rest. One Eye and Two Eyes tormented her endlessly, telling her how ugly she was because her eyes were in the wrong places. Larissa, of course, was extremely beautiful, but the two witch girls didn't know that. They thought they were the loveliest creatures on earth.

The little white goat was Larissa's only friend. Whenever Three Eyes beat her and scolded her and gave her nothing to eat but potato peelings, Larissa would go to the meadow and say to the goat,

> *"Little Goat, my only friend.*
> *Will my sorrows never end?"*

And the goat would answer,

*"Dear Larissa, you will see*
*Your every wish will come to be."*

The gentle goat would lick her bruises and give her sweet milk to make her strong. Larissa never told Three Eyes and her daughters about the wonderful talking goat, because if they knew, they would find a way to make her sufferings even worse.

One day the witch gave Larissa a basket of stinging nettles. "Card these nettles and spin them into thread. Make sure the work is done by evening, or so much the worse for you!"

"What shall I use to card them?" Larissa asked.

"Use your fingers, what else?" the old witch said.

Larissa took the basket of stinging nettles out to the meadow. "Woe is me!" she said to the goat. "Three Eyes says I must card and spin these stinging nettles into thread by evening. I cannot do it. I will be punished for sure."

"Lie down beside me on the grass," the goat said. "When you wake up, the work will be done."

Larissa lay down beside the goat and closed her eyes. She slept through the afternoon. When she awoke, all the nettles had been spun into fine thread.

The old witch could not believe her eyes when Larissa showed her the thread. "How did she manage that?" Three Eyes wondered.

The next morning, Three Eyes gave Larissa another basket of nettles. At the same time, she ordered her daughter One Eye to follow her out to the meadow and learn how the trick was done. One Eye hid behind a stone, but the little goat saw her and began to sing.

*"One Eye, sleep. One Eye, sleep. One Eye, sleep, sleep, sleep."*

One Eye closed her eye. Soon she was snoring. When she awoke, the nettles were spun into thread and Larissa was on her way home.

"Did you find out the secret?" Three Eyes asked her daughter when she returned.

"I fell asleep. When I awoke, the work was done."

"So much the worse for you!" Three Eyes screamed. She slapped One Eye until her teeth rattled and sent her to bed without any supper.

The next morning Three Eyes gave Larissa another basket of nettles. This time, she ordered Two Eyes to follow her to the meadow to find out how she spun them into thread. Two Eyes hid behind a stone, but the little goat saw her and began to sing.

*"Two eyes sleep. Two eyes sleep. Two eyes sleep, sleep, sleep."*

Two Eyes closed her eyes. Soon she was snoring. When she awoke, the nettles were spun and Larissa was on her way home.

"Did you learn how she did it?" Three Eyes asked her daughter.

"I fell asleep. When I awoke, it was all done," Two Eyes replied.

"So much the worse for you!" Three Eyes screamed. She boxed Two Eyes's ears until they turned red and threw her down in the cellar to spend the night with the rats and mice.

The next morning, Three Eyes gave Larissa another basket of nettles. Wrapping herself in Two Eyes's shawl, she followed her to the meadow. The little goat saw her coming, but seeing the shawl, she thought Two Eyes had returned. And so she sang,

*"Two Eyes, sleep. Two Eyes, sleep. Two Eyes, sleep, sleep, sleep."*

Two eyes closed. But the one in the middle of Three Eyes's forehead remained open and saw everything.

"So it is the goat who spins nettles into thread!" Three Eyes exclaimed. "I will put a stop to that."

When Larissa returned that evening, Three Eyes said, "I have discovered your trick. Say good-bye to your goat. Tomorrow morning, I will do away with her."

Larissa rushed to the meadow. She threw her arms around her little goat and told her what Three Eyes had said.

"What must be, must be, and you can do nothing to change it," the goat told Larissa. "When I am dead, the witch will cook my flesh and invite you to eat your fill. Take neither meat nor marrow, but ask for my hoofs and horns. Bury them in the far corner of the meadow and water them with your tears. Never fear. Though I am dead, I will be watching over you from heaven."

Three Eyes went to the meadow the next morning. She killed the little white goat and cut her to pieces. Her daughters cooked the meat in a pot. When it was done, they invited Larissa to eat.

"I want neither meat nor marrow," Larissa said.

"What then do you want?"

"Give me the hooves and horns."

"Take them, for all the good they will do."

Larissa took the goat's hooves and horns and buried them in the corner of the meadow. She watered the ground with her tears, which flowed from her eyes like two fountains.

When Larissa arrived at the meadow the following morning, she found a tall tree growing on that spot. Its branches bore silver leaves and golden apples. Three Eyes and her daughters came out to the meadow too, to see the wonderful tree that had grown overnight.

As they stood there, a prince came riding by. He stared at the tree and said, "I have traveled far and wide, but never have I seen a tree like this. If you will pluck one of those golden apples for me, I will grant any wish you may have."

One Eye, Two Eyes, and Three Eyes reached for the golden apples, but the branches lifted high in the air, and they could not pluck a single one.

"How is this?" the prince asked. "Can no one bring me an apple?"

"I will try," Larissa said. As she reached up, the tree lowered its branches so that the finest golden apple rested in her hand. She plucked the apple and brought it to the prince.

"Tell me your wish," he said.

"I only wish to return to my father's house," Larissa said. "I am tired of slaving for this wicked old witch and her two hideous daughters."

The prince said, "I will do that, and more. Know, beautiful maiden, that one year ago I had a dream. I dreamed that a lovely girl brought me a golden apple. I fell in love with her on the spot and swore to make her my bride. Since then, I have searched the whole world looking for her. But I need search no more, for I have found her today. You are that girl."

The prince took Larissa up on his horse and rode away.

Three Eyes raged at her daughters. "Now we have no goat and no servant! We will have to do everything ourselves. It is all the fault of this wretched tree!" She picked up a stick and struck the tree with it. A bolt of lightning arced from the sky. When the smoke and dust cleared, the tree was gone.

The old witch and her daughters were never seen again. Their house crumbled to ruins. In time, it vanished completely. The only sign that anyone had ever lived there were three black stones standing in the corner of the overgrown meadow—all that is left of One Eye, Two Eyes, and Three Eyes.